INVENTORS

THOMAS EDISON

PAUL JOSEPH
ABDO & Daughters

Published by Abdo & Daughters, 4940 Viking Drive, Suite 622, Edina, Minnesota 55435.

Copyright © 1997 by Abdo Consulting Group, Inc., Pentagon Tower, P.O. Box 36036, Minneapolis, Minnesota 55435 USA. International copyrights reserved in all countries. No part of this book may be reproduced in any form without written permission from the publisher.

Printed in the United States.

Cover illustration and icon: Kristen Copham
Interior photos: Bettmann, pages 8, 11, 16, 24, 25
        Wide World Photos, pages 5, 18, 21
        Archive Photos, page 28
Photo colorization: Professional Litho

Edited by Bob Italia

Library of Congress Cataloging-in-Publication Data

Joseph, Paul, 1970-
Thomas Edison / Paul Joseph.
  p. cm. — (Inventors)
Includes index.
Summary: Sketches the life of the "Wizard of Menlo Park," the man who patented more than one thousand inventions, the most important of which was the electric light bulb.
  ISBN 1-56239-634-X
1. Edison, Thomas A. (Thomas Alva), 1847-1931—Juvenile literature. 2. Inventors—United States—Biography—Juvenile literature. [1. Edison, Thomas A. (Thomas Alva), 1847-1931. 2. Inventors.] I. Title. II Series: Inventors (Series)
TK140.E3J74 1996
621.3'092—dc20
[B]   95-51270
                     CIP
                     AC

Contents

Thomas Edison

When Thomas Alva Edison was born, life was different than it is today. There were no televisions, radios, cars, airplanes, or movies. You could not pick up the telephone and call someone. News took months to work its way across the country.

When Thomas died, the world was much like the one we know today. Airplanes flew daily, cars lined the streets, radios carried news instantly, people could call anyone they wanted, and movies were shown across the country.

Thomas made great contributions to these **inventions**. But his greatest feat brought **electricity** to the world. Without the electricity that flows into wall sockets, we would not have televisions, radios, home computers, or other **appliances** that plug into the wall.

Thomas Edison with one of his inventions: the cylinder phonograph, 1878.

In the Beginning

Thomas Edison was born on February 11, 1847, in Milan, Ohio. He was the youngest of seven children. His father, Samuel Edison, was a **shingle** maker. His mother, Nancy Elliot Edison, was a school teacher.

As a child, Thomas was always trying new things and getting into trouble. Much of the trouble came from his **curiosity** that later would make him a great inventor.

When he was only six years old, Thomas set fire to his father's barn. He explained that he just wanted to see what the fire would do. His father gave him one of the many punishments he received as a child.

Trouble in School

When Thomas was seven years old, his family moved to Port Huron, Michigan. There, Thomas received the only formal schooling he ever had.

Thomas was not a good student. He did not like to study and he could not concentrate. He often questioned the teacher and got himself into trouble. His teacher believed that he was spoiled. This angered his mother. After three months, she took Thomas out of school and taught him at home.

Thomas' mother was a strict teacher but taught him in a loving way. He learned math, writing, and read works by William Shakespeare and Charles Dickens.

His favorite book was one his mother gave him when he was nine years old. It was a textbook on elementary science. It was full of **experiments** that he could try on his own.

Thomas Edison at 12 years old.

Smelly Bedroom Laboratory

Thomas' mother was happy with his interest in science. She bought him more science books. By the time Thomas was 10, he spent all of his spare time on **experiments**. He set up a **laboratory** in his bedroom, which quickly became a mess. He had so many foul-smelling **chemicals**, his bedroom began to smell bad. His mother made him move the laboratory to the basement.

Thomas spent much of his youth in the basement experimenting. Many of his ideas worked well, but some did not. Once he tried to make static **electricity** by attaching wires to the tails of two cats and stroking their fur! The cats did not make electricity. But they did scratch Thomas.

His First Job

Thomas got his first job selling newspapers on a train at the age of 12. The train left at seven in the morning and didn't return until nine at night.

With plenty of time on his hands, Thomas began publishing his own newspaper on the train. He used a press that printed handbills. Thomas called his newspaper *The Herald*.

Thomas published local, national, and international stories. He got his information from **telegraphers** at stations along the way. The *London Times* wrote a story about Thomas, pointing out that his newspaper was the first to be printed on a train.

Opposite page: Young Thomas Edison printing newspapers on a train.

Railroad Days End

Thomas wanted to continue his **experiments**. So, he persuaded his boss to let him build a **laboratory** on the train.

About this time, something happened that started the hearing problems which Thomas had the rest of his life. One day, he was climbing into a train car with his arms full of newspapers. Trying to help him, the conductor grabbed Thomas by the ears and lifted him into the train. Thomas felt something pop in his head, and his hearing problems began.

One day while working on an experiment, Thomas spilled some of his **chemicals**. The baggage car caught fire and filled the train with smoke. The conductor threw out Thomas and his laboratory. His railroad days had suddenly come to an end.

The Telegraph Operator

When he was 15 years old, Thomas was standing on the station platform at Mount Clemens, Michigan. Suddenly, he saw a train about to run over a child who was playing on the tracks. Thomas ran to the child and pulled him off just as the train rumbled by. The child's grateful father was the station agent. He offered to teach Thomas how to be a **telegrapher**.

At the age of 16, Thomas became a telegrapher at Stratford Junction, Canada. By the time he was 20, Thomas was the fastest telegrapher in the Midwest. He also had—and lost—14 different jobs. Sometimes he lost his job for disobeying orders. Other times, he lost jobs for building homemade gadgets to save time or work.

Full-Time Inventor

Although Thomas was an excellent **telegrapher**, he wanted to do more with his life. While working in Boston, he met a businessman who loaned him money which would allow him to work full time on his inventions.

Thomas' first invention was an automatic voting machine he designed for the U.S. **Congress**. They could vote by pressing either a yes or no button. The electronic device would then count the votes in seconds. But Congress wasn't interested at the time. They preferred their old way of roll call voting.

Twenty-four years later, the voting machine was used in the state of New York. Today, elections in many states are conducted with voting machines. They save time and prevent counting errors.

The Stock Ticker

In 1869, Thomas got a job with Western Union fixing **stock tickers**. When he developed an improved stock ticker, the company offered to pay him for this **invention**. Thomas expected only a few hundred dollars. When they handed him a check for $40,000, Thomas thought it was a joke. But the check was real—and Thomas knew exactly what to do with it.

Thomas set up a new company in Newark, New Jersey, that made stock tickers and other types of **telegraph** machines. Eventually, he had 300 workers helping him with 50 different inventions.

Before the age of 30, Thomas was a wealthy man. But because he worked so much, his health was failing. Finally, he decided to give up his Newark factory so he could regain his strength.

Thomas Edison's stock ticker machine that he sold to Western Union.

The Phonograph

When Thomas was 30, he invented something he called the "talking machine." It had a round **cylinder** wrapped in tin foil and a sharp point with a **diaphragm** and mouthpiece.

When Thomas rotated the cylinder by hand, pressed the point against the cylinder, and spoke into the mouthpiece, the sharp point **vibrated** and cut a trace into the tinfoil. When a needle replaced the sharp point and traced the lines in the tinfoil, the talking machine reproduced Thomas' words.

Thomas first demonstrated this **phonograph** to his assistants. When they heard the words "Mary had a little lamb" coming from the machine, they thought it was a trick. Eventually, everyone became convinced that the phonograph worked.

*Inventor Thomas Edison with his first phonograph,
after having worked five days and nights to perfect it.*

Family Life

Edison married Mary Stillwell in 1871. Mary had been an assistant in Thomas' **laboratory**. They had three children: Marion, Thomas, and William. Mary died in 1884.

Thomas set up a big workshop in his house where he spent most of his time. Often, his family dined alone. Thomas ate when he was hungry and slept when he was tired. He often worked 18 to 19 hours each day, not knowing when it was night or day. Thomas did not keep a clock in his workshop.

Thomas married Mina Miller in 1886. They also had three children: Madeline, Charles, and Theodore.

The Wizard
of Menlo Park

Thomas opened a **laboratory** in Menlo Park, New Jersey. There, he devoted all of his time to new **inventions**. In one year, Thomas applied for 141 **patents**, 75 of which were granted.

For the next 11 years, Thomas made many inventions that are still with us today—including the **alkaline** storage battery and telephone **transmitter**. Thomas' efforts earned him the nickname "The Wizard of Menlo Park."

Not all of his inventions came easily. Thomas worked on some for years and years and cost him a lot of money. But the effort paid off with some of the most important inventions of all time.

Thomas Edison in his laboratory, Menlo Park, New Jersey, 1898.

Thomas Edison's

1847
Born Feb. 11th in Milan, Ohio.

1860
Takes a job as a newsboy.

1863
First invention, the telegraph repeater.

1869
Patents the vote counter.

1886
Marries Mina Miller.

1887
Opens new laboratory in West Orange, New Jersey, called the Invention Factory.

1888
Invents the kinetoscope.

Detail Area

Life & Invention Timeline

1871
Marries
Mary G.
Stillwell.

1877
Invents
the
phonograph.

1879
Introduces
the light
bulb.

1913
Introduces
the first
"talking"
moving
picture.

1928
Receives the
Congressional
Gold Medal
for development
and application
of inventions.

1931
Dies Oct.
18th in
West Orange,
NJ.

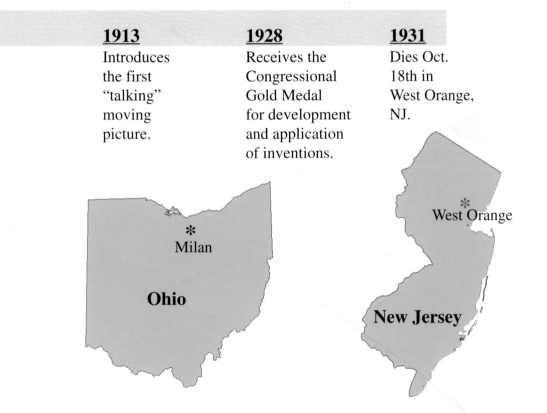

*
Milan

Ohio

*
West Orange

New Jersey

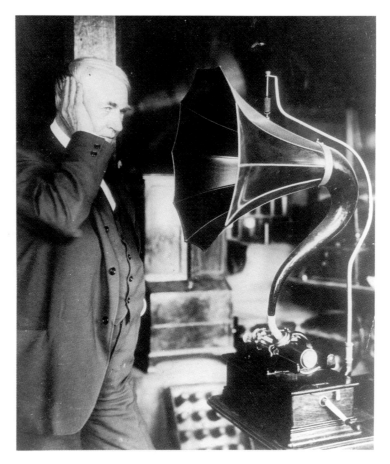

Edison listening to his phonograph in 1911.

Let There Be Light

Electricity was something scientists had been working with for many years. Thomas invented a way of using electricity to produce light.

While developing the light bulb, Thomas tried thousands of different materials for a **filament** that would work. He finally **carbonized** ordinary cotton thread by burning it. The actual filament was little more than a thread of ashes. Thread worked well, but then he discovered that **bamboo** worked better. The light bulb was finally born.

Edison's first light bulb.

Thomas wanted everyone to have electrical lighting. But for this to happen, he had to invent the electric power industry! Thomas started a company that supplied electrical power to America and Europe.

The Motion-Picture Camera

While working on the **phonograph**, Thomas also developed the motion-picture camera (the kinetograph) and projector (kinetoscope). Each used roll film developed by his friend and fellow inventor, George Eastman.

The projector was a small box inside of which the motion picture was projected. The picture was viewed through a tiny eyehole on the top of the box. Only one person could view the picture.

Eventually, Thomas developed the first motion-picture studio where movies could be made. The studio was a tar-paper shack in West Orange, New Jersey. It was built on rails so it could be moved.

The Humble Legend

In 1887, Thomas opened a new laboratory in West Orange, New Jersey. He called it the "invention factory." In addition to the light bulb, **phonograph**, and motion-picture camera, he invented a successful battery-powered automobile. He even **experimented** with flight. Thomas also improved other people's inventions, including the **telegraph**, telephone, and typewriter. In 1914, his laboratory burned down. But he continued to be productive.

Throughout his life, Thomas **patented** more inventions than any other person. Before his death at the age of 84 on October 18, 1931, Thomas was asked about all that he had accomplished. "Anyone could do it," he replied. "All they have to do is think!"

Thomas Edison in his laboratory with his light bulbs.

Glossary

alkaline battery (AL-kuh-line BAT-er-ee) - A battery that runs on acid.

appliance (uh-PLY-ants) - A household device, such as a washer or dryer.

bamboo (bam-BOO) - A tropical wood or grass with hollow stems.

carbonize (CAR-bun-eyes) - To change into carbon by burning.

chemicals (KEM-uh-kulls) - Substances used for experiments.

Congress - People who represent each state and make laws for the country.

curiosity (cure-ee-AH-sih-tee) - A desire to know things.

cylinder (SILL-un-der) - A can-shaped object.

diaphragm (DIE-uh-fram) - A disk used in converting sound to electrical impulses.

electricity (e-leck-TRISS-uh-tee) - A current or a power.

experiment (ek-SPARE-uh-ment) - The process of testing in order to discover.

filament (FILL-uh-ment) - A single thread.

invention (in-VEN-shun) - To discover or find for the first time through the use of imagination, thinking, and experimenting.

laboratory (LAB-ruh-tor-ee) - A place equipped to do experiments and study science.

patent (PAT-tent) - Owning the rights to an invention or an idea.

phonograph (FOE-no-graff) - An instrument for reproducing sounds by having a needle follow the spinal grooves of a disk.

shingle (SHING-gull)- A thin piece of wood or other materials used to cover roofs and walls.

stock ticker - A machine used by stockbrokers and other business people to print stock prices from the stock market.

telegraph (TELL-uh-graff)- A way to communicate at a distance with the use of a machine by coded signals.

telegrapher (TELL-uh-graff-er) - Someone who is trained to use a telegraph.

transmitter (trans-MITT-er) - A device that changes messages into electrical impulses that can be carried over wires.

tutored (TOO-tird) - To be taught or guided in a certain subject.

vibrate (VIE-brate) - To move back and forth or up and down rapidly.

Index

DEMCO